Drip, Drop

story by Sarah Weeks
pictures by Jane Manning

HarperCollins*Publishers*

Drip, Drop
Text copyright © 2000 by Sarah Weeks
Illustrations copyright © 2000 by Jane Manning
Printed in the U.S.A. All rights reserved.
www.harperchildrens.com

Library of Congress Catalog Card Number: 00-21652
ISBN 0-06-028523-0. — ISBN 0-06-028524-9 (lib. bdg.)
1 2 3 4 5 6 7 8 9 10
❖
First Edition

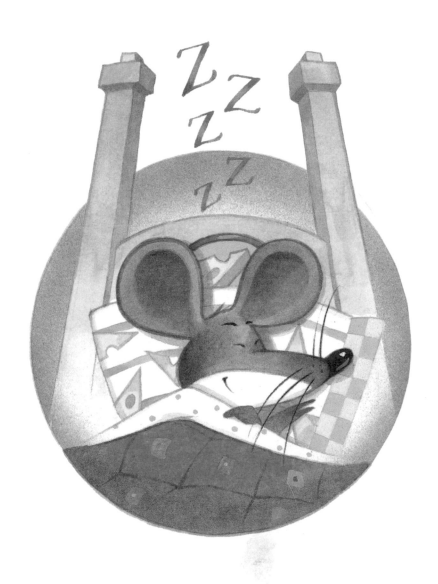

Pip Squeak lay in his bed.

Something wet fell

on his head.

Drip! Drop!

Plip! Plop!

"Oh, no!" cried Pip Squeak.

"I've got a leak!"

He climbed up

and got a cup.

"This cup will do the trick,"

he said.

Off he went, back to bed.

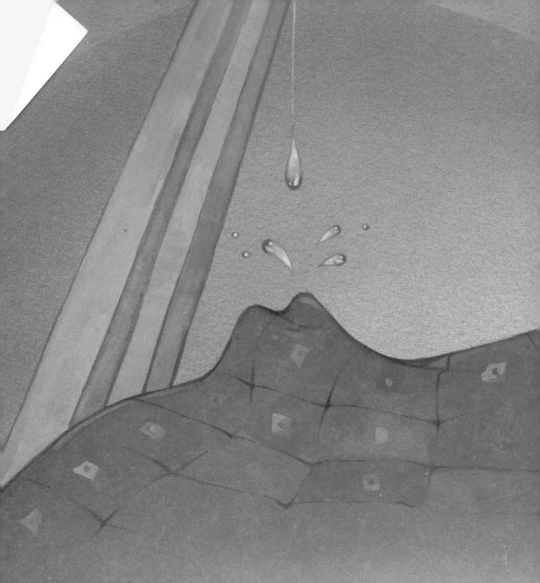

His eyes had just begun to close.

Then something wet

fell on his toes.

Drip! Drop!

Plip! Plop!

"Oh, no!" cried Pip Squeak.

"I've got a new leak."

Away he ran
to get a pan.

"This pan will do the trick,"

he said.

Off he went, back to bed.

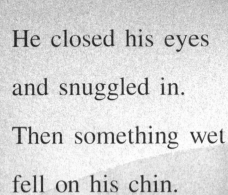

He closed his eyes

and snuggled in.

Then something wet

fell on his chin.

Drip! Drop!

Plip! Plop!

"Oh, no!" cried Pip Squeak.

"I've got another leak."

He went and got
a great big pot.

"This pot will do the trick,"

he said.

Off he went, back to bed.

Thunder boomed!

Lightning flashed!

A new leak splished,
another splashed.

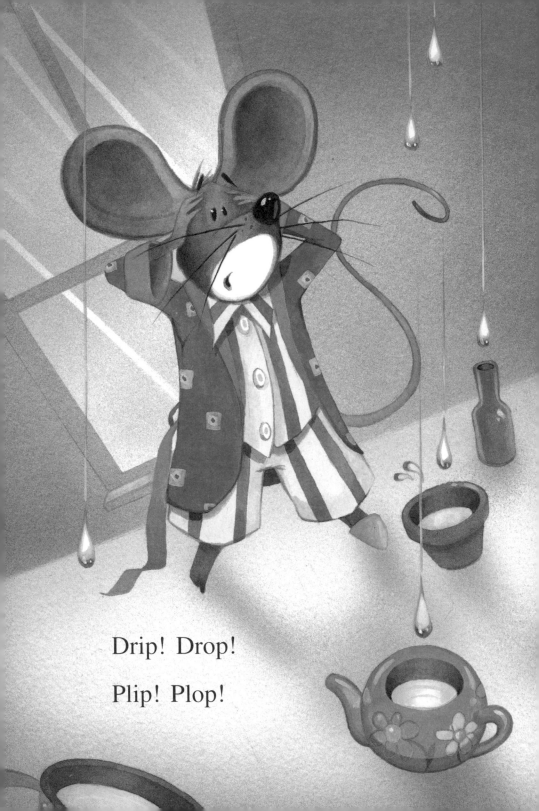

Drip! Drop!

Plip! Plop!

Down came the rain.

It would not stop.

It filled the pot.

It filled the pan.

It filled the cup.

It filled the can.

It filled the pail,

and after that

it filled the glass.

It filled the hat.

It filled the tub.

It filled the shoe.

Pip Squeak did not know
what to do!

There was nothing left
to catch the drips or drops
or plips or plops.

"I give up," said Pip Squeak.

"Just go ahead and leak!"

He hung his head
and closed his eyes.
Then Pip Squeak
had a big surprise.

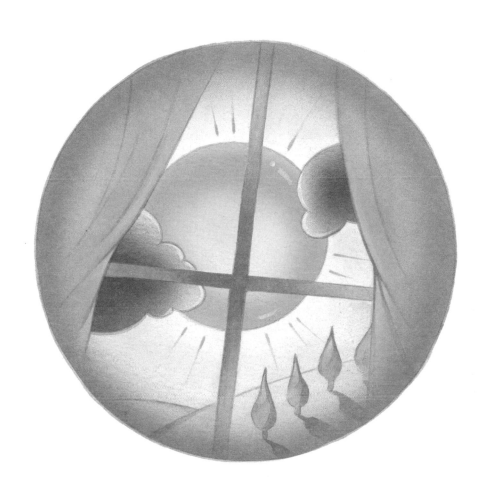

The sun came out.

The rain had stopped.

No drops dripped.

No plips plopped.

"Come jump in the puddles,"

his friends all said.

But Pip Squeak ran

and jumped in . . .

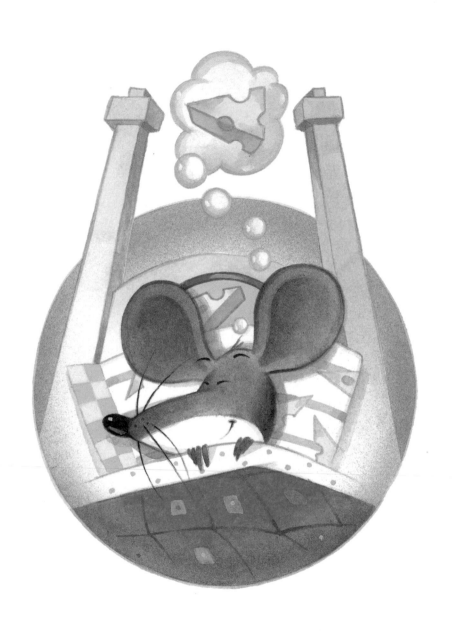

. . . bed.